gru

m P^s

allowed!

by Janet S. Wong

illustrated by

John Wallace

Margaret K. McElderry Books

New York   London   Toronto   Sydney   Singapore

Margaret K. McElderry Books
An imprint of Simon & Schuster Children's Publishing Division
1230 Avenue of the Americas
New York, New York 10020

Book design by Lee Wade and Ann Bobco
The text of this book is set in Adobe Caslon.
The illustrations were rendered in watercolor.

Printed in Hong Kong

2 4 6 8 10 9 7 5 3

Library of Congress Cataloging-in-Publication Data
Wong, Janet S.
Grump / by Janet S. Wong; illustrated by John Wallace.   p.   cm.
Summary: A very tired and slightly grumpy Mommy falls asleep before Baby
at naptime.
ISBN 0-689-83485-3
[1. Mothers—Fiction. 2. Babies—Fiction. 3. Naps (Sleep)—Fiction. 4. Stories in rhyme.]
I. Wallace, John, 1966- ill. II. Title.
PZ8.3.W8465 Gr 2001 [E]—dc21   99-59545

To Andrew and Glenn,
who know how grumpy this *Mommy gets*
—*J. S. W.*

To Polly (who is never grumpy)
—*J. W.*

Look how tired this Mommy is

Tired and frumpy

Grouchy chumpy

Oh, what a grump!

Look at Baby
Smart, good Baby
Happy Baby

Making gravy
Applesauce and ketchup gravy

Not too lumpy

Not too bumpy

Squish squish

DUMP!

Mommy's stomping

Jumping, chomping

Long arms dragging like a chimp.

Sponging all the spots away
Wash and wash and wash
All day.

Mommy's slumping

 Mommy's tired

Thump
Thump
Thumping
up the stairs.

Grumpy heavy stump-thump thumping

Baby's going to take
a nap now

Baby's going to take
a nap now

Baby's going to take a nap now

Take a nap now

Little lump.

Mommy dumps her baby g e n t l y

Dumps him gently in the crib

Drums on Baby's rump *pum pum pum!*

Rubs his back

Plump arms

Plump legs

Baby's eyes are getting heavy
Heavy sleepy baby eyes

Mommy starts to tiptoe out–

And oh of course that baby cries

Cries and whimpers

Cries and whimpers

Cries and whimpers

Play with me!

So Mommy sits
And reads to Baby
Reads so pretty
Reads so softly

Reads and reads and reads until—

There's no sound
· Except the wind

There's no sound
Except the trees

And Baby looks

And Baby looks

And Baby looks

And Baby sees

Mommy's slumping, crumpled, sleeping
Fast asleep in her big chair
Mommy's fast asleep
   already?

Sleeping, sleeping
Sleeping near

Look at Baby

Smart, good Baby

Happy Baby curling up
Curling up so tired
Tired

Precious

Little Baby

Lump–

No more

No more

No more GRUMP.